C. Morison

And Then It Happened
..7..

From the personal
library of
Mrs. Lindsay Spence

W9-CDL-816

AND THEN IT HAPPENED

HAPPENED

.. 7 ..

M & L Wade

Books for Boys

ISBN 10 digit 0-9731178-6-9
ISBN 13 digit 978-0973117868

Printed in Canada

Books For Boys Inc.
P.O. Box 87
Strathroy ON N7G 3J1

Contents

Chapter 1

Another Good Deed

What started out as a beautiful hot summer day turned out to be one of the grossest days of the year. Gordon, Paulo and I had spent all day fishing at the river. The fish were biting and we were having a lot of fun, but all good things must come to an end. By five o'clock we were tired and hungry and it was time to head home and clean up for dinner. As we biked up the hill toward town, we passed a small house with a big yard. A little old lady was struggling to push her lawnmower up and down the steep hills of her lawn. We could see her frail body straining and sweating under the hot afternoon sun. We slowed down to a stop and watched.

"Gee," Gordon said. "Look at that. She's way too old to be mowing her own lawn, especially on such a hot day. Do you think we have time to help her and still make it home in time for dinner?"

I looked at my watch. If we hurried, we could probably make it. We pedalled up her long driveway and waved hello. The old woman saw us and shut off the mower. She smiled at us and we noticed right away that the old woman had no teeth. Gordon introduced us and said that we would like to finish cutting her lawn for her. At first I thought she was going to refuse our help, but then she gave us a gummy grin and said, "That would be wonderful! But I'm afraid I can't pay you. I don't have much money."

"Oh, we don't want any money," said Gordon quickly. "We'd be happy to do it for free. On a hot day like this you should be resting in the shade, not pushing a heavy lawnmower."

The old lady nodded in appreciation. As Gordon started up the mower and began cutting the lawn, Paulo and I sat in the shade on the front porch chatting with the woman, who was a little hard of hearing.

After several minutes, I took Gordon's place pushing the mower while he sat with Paulo and the woman on the shady porch. When I thought I couldn't take the heat much longer, Paulo came and took his turn. As Gordon and I sat on the porch talking to the old lady, my stomach rumbled loudly and sweat dripped from my forehead.

Noticing how hot and sweaty we were, the old lady insisted on going into the house to make us some lemonade. Paulo finished cutting the lawn and joined us on the front porch. We waited for the old lady to return with the lemonade. My stomach rumbled again.

"I wonder what's taking so long?" I asked, looking at my watch. "We've got to get home for dinner. I'm starving."

Spying a bowl of peanuts on the table beside him, Gordon reached out and helped himself to a few, saying, "I'm sure she won't mind."

Paulo and I helped ourselves to the peanuts as well, and before we knew it, we had eaten most of the bowl. I guess we had all been starving.

"These peanuts are really good," said Gordon, grabbing another handful.

At last the old lady returned with three glasses and a pitcher of lemonade on a tray.

"I'm so sorry," said Gordon. "My friends and I were really hungry and we helped ourselves to the peanuts. Right after supper, we'll go to the store and buy you another bag."

"Oh, don't worry about that," said the woman as she poured three tall glasses of lemonade for us.

"No, really," insisted Gordon. "We shouldn't have helped ourselves without asking. It's just that it's almost dinnertime and we spent the entire day at the river fishing and we were starving."

"I don't mind at all," she said kindly. "You just help yourselves."

"Thanks!" we chorused, reaching into the bowl. And then it happened. As we hungrily munched the last of the peanuts, the old lady sighed and said, "You see, ever since I lost all my teeth, I can only suck the chocolate off them, anyway!"

Chapter 2

The Stampede

One sunny autumn day, Gordon, Paulo and I found ourselves in the emergency room at the hospital, along with our principal, most of our teachers and a dozen students from school. Fortunately, no one was seriously hurt; we just had minor cuts, bruises and sprains. Gordon, Paulo and I were the last to be seen by the doctor. As he stitched up a cut on Gordon's arm he said, "So you're the kids who were responsible for getting everyone caught up in that stampede!"

"What? Us?!" we cried out.

"We didn't do anything wrong!" added Gordon.

"That's not what your principal said," chuckled the doctor. "Or your teacher. And all those kids I bandaged up."

"It wasn't our fault," insisted Gordon. "Here's what *really* happened."

$$* \quad * \quad * \quad * \quad *$$

A new pet store had recently opened in town. As part of its grand opening celebration, the owners were sponsoring a pet talent contest for the students of our school. Entry was free, and the owner of the pet that did the best trick would win a two hundred dollar grand prize. Two hundred dollars is a lot of money and Gordon, Paulo and I decided right then and there that we were going to win the grand prize!

All of the students were given entry forms with the rules printed on the back. Gordon, Paulo and I filled in our names and carefully read the rules.

"Hmmm," said Gordon. "It says the teachers are going to judge the talent show."

"And the pets will be judged on two things," added Paulo. "Originality of the trick, and difficulty of the trick."

"Well," I said. "We'll have to come up with something so original and so difficult that even the teachers won't have seen it before." Paulo and I both turned to Gordon and waited. We were depending on him to come up with something really spectacular and show stopping.

Gordon did not let us down. By the end of the school day, he had come up with a plan that was truly original and sure to win the two hundred dollar grand prize. As we rode home with Paulo on the bus to the Lima family farm, he outlined his plan and, once again, Paulo and I were impressed.

When the bus reached the farm, we hurried off and raced toward the cow pasture. Now, everyone knows that cows are not at the head of the line when it comes to animal intelligence. As a matter of fact, most people would agree that cows are pretty dumb creatures.

"You see," reasoned Gordon. "If we can teach a bunch of dumb cows to do a really cool trick, we'll win that prize for sure!"

With just one week until the contest, there was no time to waste. We separated what we believed were the ten smartest looking cows from the rest of the herd, and put them in their own special field. We worked for three hours every day after school to train them. It was the hardest work we had ever done. It took two days of sweating and grunting just to teach the ten cows to stand in a straight line, side by side, on command. It took another day to get them to sit down on command. Next came the real trick. Gordon stood in front of the line of sitting cows and pulled a bell from his pocket. He rang it once, and the cows, with much poking and prodding from Paulo and me, stood up. Then Gordon rang the bell twice and the cows began to walk slowly toward Gordon's outstretched hand, which held some lovely fresh alfalfa as a reward. Gordon then rang the bell three times and the cows trotted toward the end of the pasture where they all sat down, still in their nice neat line. It was a fantastic trick!

Day after day we practised and soon the cows were trained to perform the trick without any reward from Gordon, or any poking and prodding from Paulo and me. They became conditioned to the sound of the bell and responded eagerly when they heard it. On the first ring, the ten cows would rise gracefully from their sitting position. Patiently they'd wait until Gordon rang the bell twice. Then the line of cows would walk slowly toward him. When Gordon rang the bell three times, the cows picked up their pace and trotted toward him. When he held up his hands, the cows all sat down again, still in their neat line. It was a beautiful trick, guaranteed to win the two hundred dollar grand prize.

Finally, the day of the pet contest arrived. At two o'clock, the students were told to go home and bring their pets back to where the contest would take place in the soccer field behind the playground. Gordon, Paulo and I hopped on our bikes and pedalled quickly to the Lima farm. We got the cows to sit in their line and Gordon rang the bell once. The cows stood up and waited expectantly. Gordon rang the bell twice and the cows moved slowly toward Gordon. He rang it three times and the cows trotted toward Gordon. The cows followed us down the long driveway, onto the road and right into town. Fifteen minutes later we arrived at school and led the cows to the back of the schoolyard where they sat down in the shade to rest.

While we waited for our turn in the pet talent show, we joined the rest of the spectators. Chairs had been set up in two rows for the teachers who would judge the contest. The kids who were not participating in the contest sat on the grass to one side of the teachers, while all those with pets sat on the other side. For half an hour we watched as dogs were paraded in front of the teachers and made to sit, lie down and roll over. A few played dead and one toy poodle even did somersaults. The teachers clapped politely and graded each pet on its performance. There was a cat that could walk on his hind legs, a lizard whose only trick was sticking out his blue tongue to capture crickets, and a budgie that could sing the first line of the national anthem. Gordon, Paulo and I grinned at each other. There was no way any of these tricks could come close to beating us. That prize money was as good as ours!

Since our pets were the largest by far, our trick had been left to the end of the show. When our turn finally came, we herded the cows to within thirty metres of the teachers and made them lie down in their neat row. So far, so good. We stood beside Gordon as he rang the bell once. The cows stood up in unison. This brought murmurs of approval from the teachers and applause from the students. Gordon rang the bell twice and the cows all marched slowly forward. Then he rang it three times and the cows began to trot. By now, everyone was very impressed and it was clear that we had the most difficult and original trick in the show. Mrs. Hoagsbrith looked proud that three of *her* students had such an amazing trick.

* * * * *

"And then it happened," Gordon told the doctor who was stitching up his arm.

"And then *what* happened?" asked the doctor.

"Well," said Gordon wistfully. "If that darn ice-cream truck hadn't come speeding by, ringing its bell like crazy, we would have won that contest for sure!"

Chapter 3

Halloween

There are three certainties in every kid's life: homework, chores, and the year your parents tell you you're too old to go out for Halloween. This year, none of the kids in our class were allowed to go trick-or-treating. Most of us were assigned the boring task of handing out candy at the door instead of the excitement of *collecting* candy door-to-door. Gordon, Paulo and I were especially upset by the fact that our parents expected us to hand out candy this year. We reminded our parents that in the last three years, we had not collected a single chocolate bar, bag of chips or pack of gum between the three of us. If there were any justice in the world, we argued, our parents would not deny us one last chance to go trick-or-treating. Apparently, there is no justice in the world. Our parents held firm.

"You're too old for trick-or-treating," they told us. "This year, you're handing out candy, and that's final!"

We knew better than to argue with our parents when their minds were made up; besides, Paulo and I figured that Gordon would come up with a plan to get us out of handing out candy and collecting some for ourselves. We were not disappointed!

"Listen," said Gordon the next day at recess. "This may be our final chance to go out for Halloween. We can't let our parents rob us of the opportunity to get lots of candy. After all, we deserve it!"

Paulo and I agreed and waited eagerly for Gordon to tell us his plan.

"We're supposed to go to Paulo's house and hand out candy, right?" asked Gordon.

"Right," said Paulo. "My parents are going to a party so they can't do it."

"Mine, too," I said. "But my sister and her friend are handing out the candy at my place."

"OK," said Gordon. "We'll go to Paulo's and hand out his candy, but as soon as we're done, we'll get into our costumes and take off trick-or-treating."

"How are we going to sneak costumes out of the house without our parents getting suspicious?" I asked.

"Yeah. I don't want to get into trouble again," added Paulo.

"That's the beauty of this plan. We can't possibly get caught," Gordon assured us. "Not only will we hand out all the candy at Paulo's house, but we're going to collect a ton of candy for ourselves, too. When people see the great costume I have in mind for the three of us, they will *throw* the candy at us by the bowlful. And we won't even have to utter a single 'trick-or-treat' or ring any doorbells. We'll honestly be able to tell our parents that we *didn't* go trick-or-treating."

"What do you mean *'the costume you have in mind for the three of us'*?" I asked suspiciously, picturing myself stuck in the rear end of a horse costume or something.

"You'll see," said Gordon. "Meet me at my place after school and we'll get started on it."

I spent the rest of the day wondering what Gordon had in mind. When he finally told us his plan, I had to admit it was brilliant!

"Gordon, you've outdone yourself," I said, and we quickly set to work.

First, we bolted two old wooden wagons together to make one large one. Then we removed the front and back wheels and replaced them with tires from our bikes to raise the wagon up off of the ground. Next, we measured Gordon and cut up some old plywood Gordon had found in his basement. We hammered the pieces together, painted it black, and then stood back to admire our work – one coffin on wheels!

"And now to try it out," said Gordon, climbing in and laying down. He closed his eyes and folded his hands upon his chest.

"Cool," I said.

"Creepy," whispered Paulo. "You really look dead lying there."

"Perfect!" exclaimed Gordon, climbing out. "And you guys will make great pallbearers dressed in your suits."

Halloween was just two days away. In order to keep our parents from getting suspicious, we all whined and pouted about missing our last chance to go trick-or-treating. They still didn't change their minds.

October 31st finally arrived. At ten minutes to six, I stuffed my only suit, a white shirt and one of my dad's ties into my backpack and at six o'clock sharp I was dropped off at Paulo's house.

"Bye, dad," I mumbled, trying my best to look sad and disappointed.

"Cheer up!" he told me. "It won't be so bad handing out candy. You might actually enjoy it."

To my surprise, he was right. It felt great dumping the entire bowl of candy into the pillowcase of the first trick-or-treater to knock on Paulo's door. The kid thanked us with a huge grin before he ran off, lugging his heavy load.

"Well, we gave out all the candy, just like my parents told us to," said Paulo, turning out the porch light and blowing out the pumpkin. "Now it's *our* turn to get some loot!"

We quickly got into our suits. Gordon had purchased a skullcap and some bushy white eyebrows at a costume shop to make him look like an old man. He covered his face with white powder. The effect was fantastic. Lying motionless in the coffin with his arms folded across his chest, Gordon really looked like a dead 80-year-old man. Paulo and I walked on opposite sides of the coffin and tried to look sad as we wheeled Gordon toward town.

Careful to stay away from our own neighbourhood where we might be recognized, we walked down street

19

after street, Gordon playing dead while Paulo and I acted as mournful pallbearers. When people saw us passing by, they came out of their houses for a better look. Delighted and surprised by our ingenious costume, they ran back inside to get handful after handful of candy for us, which they dropped into the coffin around Gordon. Before long, the coffin was brimming with candy, chips and chocolate bars. A few people even snapped our picture as we marched along.

We were nearing the wealthy end of town, where they always give out the best candy. Paulo and I struggled to push the coffin, which had grown heavier with candy, up the steep hill toward the mansions at the top.

"Come on, guys," urged Gordon.

"We're almost at the top," panted Paulo, and then it happened.

Paulo tripped in a pothole and lost his grip on the coffin. I tried desperately to keep the coffin from rolling back down the steep hill, but loaded down with Gordon and all of our candy, it was just too heavy.

"NO!" I yelled, as the coffin rolled down the hill, picking up speed at an alarming rate.

Paulo was back on his feet and the two of us raced after Gordon.

"STOP THAT COFFIN!" I yelled. By now Gordon was sitting up and candy was flying out in all directions. Kids came from out of nowhere, running to stop the coffin and save Gordon. At least that's what I *thought* they were doing. Then I saw them scrambling and grabbing at the candy that littered the road – *our candy!*

"They're stealing our candy!" I shouted.

"Never mind that! Gordon's headed straight for the river!" yelled Paulo.

Sure enough, Gordon, and what was left of our candy, flew across the road at the foot of the hill and plunged right into the river on the other side! On impact, the coffin tore loose from the wagons upon which it sat. The wagons immediately sank, but the coffin began floating down the river, taking Gordon with it!

Paulo and I plunged into the chilly water and swam after the coffin. We had just caught up with it when we suddenly heard the wail of fire engines in the distance. Someone had called the fire department and they were racing to the river to save us! A minute later a huge searchlight blinded us and a voice boomed out, "Stay with your craft. We are coming to rescue you."

"Oh, no," moaned Paulo, gripping the side of the coffin as we floated down the river. "I just knew it was too good to be true. Your stupid plan got us into trouble *again*, Gordon!"

"Relax," said Gordon. "Our parents will never find out."

A rope was thrown to us from the rescue squad on shore, and we were pulled to safety, Gordon sitting in the coffin and Paulo and I floating alongside. As Gordon stepped from the coffin, a news camera from the local TV station zeroed in on all three of us.

*   *   *   *   *

Meanwhile, back in town, Gordon's parents were watching the nine o'clock news. They tuned in just in time to see their son's face filling the screen as he spoke to the rescue squad.

"We're fine," Gordon assured them. "But whatever you do, *please don't tell our parents!"*

Chapter 4

When Girls Attack

It was a rainy, gray Monday morning just after announcements when our teacher stood up and said, "Well, I have an announcement of my own. You will all be happy to learn that I volunteered our class to put together this year's school yearbook! It will be a lot of fun for everyone." She beamed at us. I sank deep into my chair. I learned a long time ago that what teachers say and what students hear are two entirely different things. What the class actually heard went more like this: "You will all be unhappy to know that I am ordering you to put together this year's school yearbook. It will be a lot of extra work for everyone."

As well, what teachers see is often different from what students see. I looked around the room and saw rows of grief-stricken students. Mrs. Hoagsbrith no doubt saw row after row of smiling eager beavers!

Next, our teacher organized the class into eight separate groups and began handing out "the fun." To my surprise, Mrs. Hoagsbrith let Gordon, Paulo and me form our own group. We were put in charge of photographing all of the staff at Danglemore Public School. She handed each of us a small disposable camera and told us that we should use our imaginations to try and make this year's yearbook unique. She didn't want the same boring pictures that were in every other yearbook.

Gordon, Paulo and I looked at each other in surprise. Was she kidding? Did Mrs. Hoagsbrith forget whom she was talking to? Was she actually giving *Gordon* permission to use his imagination on an important school project? For once our teacher was right! This *was* going to be fun!!

We decided that instead of taking the staff's pictures in stiff, formal poses, we were going to take surprise snapshots of the staff in totally zany and candid poses. We would catch the teachers by surprise and snap their pictures before they even knew what was happening! I was going to love this assignment.

We plotted our strategy on how to take the funniest pictures. For two hours that night we wrote down our ideas and formulated a plan. It was the first time I can honestly say I spent two whole hours on homework.

Gordon figured the hardest picture to get would be of our principal, Mr. Evans, since he had no sense of humour at all and rarely did anything spontaneous or funny. We therefore decided to make the principal our first target.

Early the next morning, Gordon, Paulo and I snuck into the school to get ready.

When Mr. Evans walked into his private office a half hour later, he found Gordon sitting in his chair with his feet on the desk. He was reading the principal's newspaper and an unlit cigar dangled from his mouth.

"Hey, knock before you come in here!" ordered Gordon.

Mr. Evans turned the brightest shade of red and yelled in his loudest voice, "GORDON SMITH!! WHAT DO YOU THINK YOU'RE DOING??"

At that exact moment, Paulo jumped out and snapped his picture. "Thanks," he said politely. "We needed that for the yearbook."

Mr. Evans sighed. "OK, kids, you got me. Now go outside and wait for the bell to ring."

*　　*　　*　　*　　*

Our next target was our gym teacher, Mr. Sax. Unfortunately for him, someone had discovered that Mr. Sax's first name was Jim. Ever since then, he has been *"Gym Socks"* to the whole school. Gym Socks must have weighed over 300 pounds and was probably the fattest gym teacher in the history of gym teachers. Everyone in school was used to the sight of the hefty teacher eating jelly donuts before, during and between classes. We figured he ate about two dozen donuts a day. In addition to being a big fan of jelly donuts, Gym Socks was also a huge fan of the Toronto Maple Leafs. I don't think there's ever been a bigger Leaf fan in the team's history. It was rumoured that Gym Socks failed kids simply for showing up to class in a Montreal Canadiens shirt.

When our class arrived at the gym at 11:30, I peeked into Gym Socks' office and as usual, he was eating a jelly donut and reading The Hockey News. Paulo and I went to the far end of the gym and on cue, I yelled at Paulo,

"My dad says the Detroit Red Wings are the best team in the league!"

"No way!" returned Paulo. "*My* dad says the Canadiens are the best team in the NHL!"

It was like waving a red flag in front of a bull. Gym Socks snapped to attention, choking on the jelly donut he had just popped into his mouth. He leapt out of his chair and lumbered across the gym to where Paulo and I stood. He shouted statistic after statistic to us, proving beyond all doubt that the Toronto Maple Leafs were the best team in the history of organized sports.

As Paulo and I listened to the teacher going on and on about his favourite team, Gordon went to work. Sneaking into Gym Socks' office, he carefully squeezed out all of the jelly from the six remaining donuts in the box and neatly filled each hole with mustard.

By the time Gym Socks finished explaining to Paulo and me how the Maple Leafs were the best team in the NHL and how our fathers clearly knew nothing about hockey, he was panting and sweaty and in desperate need of a jelly donut. He headed straight back to his office, dropped into his chair and grabbed one out of the box. He tore off a huge bite and chewed two or three times before the taste hit him. His entire face curled into the world's biggest pucker! At that exact instant, Gordon jumped out of the supply closet and snapped his picture. The photo turned out great! We quickly explained that we were taking candid shots of everyone on staff for the yearbook. Even Gym Socks laughed when we assured him that his six donuts would be replaced.

As the week progressed, we surprised teacher after teacher and got great pictures for the yearbook. By Friday, the only staff members that we hadn't been able to capture in a funny pose were our two female custodians. We tried many times to surprise them, but they were battle hardened from years of cleaning up after kids, and nothing we did could shock them. Finally, Gordon came up with a foolproof plan.

We had noticed that the last room the custodians cleaned every day was the girls' change room. When school ended on Friday, volleyball practice began. Gordon, Paulo and I hid around the corner and carefully counted the number of players as they went into the change room and then came out again for practice. There were 18 girls on the team. Fifty minutes later, practice ended and the team filed back into the change room. Another quarter of an hour later we counted as the last girl left the change room.

We quickly ran up to the door and knocked on it, just to be on the safe side. No one answered, so Gordon called out, "Hello. Anybody in there?" He was answered with silence.

"The coast is clear," he said. "Let's go." Taking one last look over our shoulders to make sure we hadn't been spotted, we ducked into the girls' change room. Clutching our cameras, we hid in three separate lockers and waited for the custodians to arrive.

Five minutes later we could hear them coming down the hall. They were talking and giggling about something, but it was impossible to hear what they were saying from inside the lockers. A minute later the door opened and they came into the change room.

They sure are making a lot of noise for just two ladies, I thought.

As planned, we waited for Gordon to give us the signal to jump out and startle the custodians and then snap their picture.

"Now!" he yelled. All three of us burst out of our lockers, the flashes on our cameras going off simultaneously, and then it happened. Instantly, the room

31

was filled with screaming, kicking, scratching girls! We had no idea that the girls' field hockey team from the high school used our field for practice every Friday afternoon!

We never got the chance to explain about our yearbook assignment. Our cameras were torn from our hands and smashed on the ground. We were chased out of the locker room by a team of hockey stick-swinging high school girls!

Gordon, Paulo and I limped home to lick our wounds and to begin our yearbook assignment all over again.

Chapter 5

Dashing Through the Snow

Nothing ruins Christmas more than endless reminders about the poor, the hungry and the homeless. Gordon, Paulo and I have noticed that whenever someone invents something great like Christmas, which makes people happy and cheerful, certain other people (like teachers and principals) won't rest until everyone is unhappy and cheerless again, worrying about the poor, the hungry and the homeless. Their usual method of ruining the holiday is to constantly remind us of those less fortunate than ourselves. The teachers at our school are pros at this.

Mr. Evans, our principal, called a special assembly early in December. He announced that this year, instead

33

of constructing a school float to enter in the town's annual Christmas parade, our school would save the money and donate it to a shelter for homeless people. Instead of spending money decorating our school, we would donate the money to a food bank. Furthermore, Mr. Evans announced that on December 19th, our school would be hosting a special fund-raising dinner for all the important people in town. All the money raised would be given to a poor family to buy presents for their kids. Clearly pleased with himself, our principal beamed at us. I don't know if he expected applause or cheering, but he was met with silence – unhappy, cheerless silence.

At recess, there was much groaning and grumbling in the playground. Everyone knew that hosting the charity dinner would mean lots of extra work for us students. We would be expected to wait on tables, to greet the guests at the door, and to clean up afterwards, including washing mountains of dirty dishes. Tables and chairs would have to be set up and taken down afterwards, and the gym floor would have to be swept and washed.

34

"This is exactly the sort of thing we've been talking about," complained Paulo. "When you put the principal in charge of something like Christmas, it's good-bye, fun. Hello, work!"

"It's like putting a dentist in charge of Halloween," I agreed. "Good-bye, candy. Hello, toothbrush."

"Or a hunter in charge of Groundhog Day," continued Gordon. "Hello, hunter. BANG! Good-bye, groundhog!"

We spent the rest of the day feeling sorry for ourselves and complaining about the lack of justice in the world.

A few days later, a sign was posted in the front hall of the school with a list of jobs for everyone. Gordon, Paulo and I got off easy compared to some students. We were assigned the job of placing signs advertising the fund-raising dinner around town. We hung them at the Post Office, the grocery store, and on telephone poles where people would see them.

December 19th finally arrived. Mrs. Hoagsbrith cornered Gordon, Paulo and me and said that since we had been assigned such an easy job, she had another task for us. At five o'clock that afternoon, we were expected to show up at school and sit by the gym doors to sell tickets for the charity dinner.

Arriving a few minutes before five, we noticed that a table and three chairs had been set up for us by the gym doors. There was a cashbox sitting on the table for us to put the money in.

"This shouldn't be too bad," said Paulo. "Dinner starts at six o'clock, so we should be done selling tickets in an hour."

Soon, all the important people in town started showing up for the charity dinner: the mayor, the chief of police, some rich bankers, and most of the kids' parents from school. It was a great turnout and by the time dinner began, we had sold nearly two thousand dollars worth of tickets.

"Wow! That family we're giving all this money to is sure going to have a nice Christmas," said Gordon.

"Yeah," agreed Paulo. "I'll bet that without all this

money, their kids would get nothing on Christmas morning."

We locked the money in the cashbox and decided to take it with us for safekeeping to our classroom. We were going to play computer games to kill the time until the dinner was over and we could give the money to our principal.

Before we knew it, a couple of hours passed. Shutting off the computer, we picked up the cashbox and headed back to the gym. To our surprise, it was almost empty. About a dozen kids were stacking chairs and tables and carrying out the garbage.

"Hey, where's Mr. Evans?" asked Gordon.

"He left a few minutes ago. All of the teachers were heading over to the mayor's house for a party after the dinner," one of the students informed us.

"Oh, great," sighed Gordon. "What are we supposed to do with all this money?"

"Well, we know where the mayor lives. We could take the money over there and give it to Mr. Evans," I suggested.

"I guess we've got no choice," agreed Gordon and Paulo. We put on our coats and boots and headed off through the dark, snowy night to the mayor's house at the opposite end of town. Gordon carried the heavy cashbox under his arm.

We hadn't gone more than half a block when a black car with two men inside it pulled up beside us. A window rolled down and the passenger called out, "Hey, can you tell me where the nearest gas station is?"

"Sure," said Gordon, approaching the car. "You just go to the end of the street and turn right..." Without warning, the passenger's arm shot out of the window and grabbed at the cashbox!

"Hey!" yelped Gordon, yanking it away and leaping away from the car.

"Give us the money, if you know what's good for you!" snarled the man angrily as he opened the door and climbed out. He was a huge man and he didn't look friendly.

"Run!" I yelled, and Gordon, Paulo and I turned and ran for it. The man chased us down the block while the black car sped past us and stopped half a block in front of us. The driver leapt out of the car and came at us from the other direction. We were cut off! Veering to the right, we raced up a driveway, hopped a fence and tore across someone's backyard. Climbing over another fence, we found ourselves near the school and decided to run back for help. As I stole a glance over my shoulder, I could see the big man still chasing us, and when we ran into the schoolyard, the black car pulled into the parking lot, cutting us off again!

Not ready to give up, we turned and dashed through the snow. Climbing another fence, we raced down the street. The man and the black car were hot on our trail.

I guess we could have given up and just handed over the money, but the thought of that poor family losing their only chance at a decent Christmas was too much. We had to protect the money at all costs and get away from the thieves.

Three times we thought we'd lost the thieves, and three times they turned up right on our heels. Hiding behind the corner of a house, Gordon whispered, "I think we've lost them for now. Listen, I've got an idea."

Exhausted from running and hopping fences, I was willing to try anything, even one of Gordon's crazy ideas.

"See that church across the road?" he asked, pointing. "Look at the nativity scene on the front lawn. I'll bet those Wise Men's costumes would fit us."

Without waiting to hear the rest of the plan, we all darted across the road and began pulling the clothes off of the Wise Men. We quickly slipped the robes over our coats and put on the fake beards and crowns. Then, carrying gold, frankincense and the cashbox, we stood motionless on the church lawn, hoping that the thieves would give up once they realized they had lost us.

A few minutes passed and then we heard a car cruising slowly by. It stopped and two men got out. It was the thieves!

"Where do you think they got to?" one of them

asked, standing less than a metre away from our frozen figures.

"I don't know, but their tracks end here, so they've gotta be around here someplace," said the second man. Despite the cold, sweat trickled down my back and I waited for them to recognize us.

"Well, they're not here!" said the first man. "They must have circled back. Get in the car and let's keep searching!"

The minute the car was out of sight, Gordon gasped, "That was too close! Let's get this cashbox to my house, fast!"

We took off in the direction of Gordon's house. As we ran down the street, we could hear a car getting closer.

"Quick! Over here," hissed Gordon, running onto someone's front lawn and striking a pose. Paulo and I got in line behind him and stood as still as possible while the black car slowly made its way down the street in search of us. It slowed as it passed us, but sped off as the thieves saw what appeared to be just another Christmas display of the Three Wise Men. Once it rounded the corner, we raced toward Gordon's house, stopping to pose on someone's lawn whenever we heard the car approaching. Four times we were able to outwit the thieves, but the fifth time they passed us standing motionless in the middle of someone's lawn, the car slowed down and stopped. The window slowly rolled down and the driver stuck his head out.

"Hey, wait a minute! These lawn decorations are startin' to look awfully familiar," he said. The words were barely out of his mouth, and then it happened. Gordon sneezed! In an instant the men were out of the car and the chase was on!

We were exhausted and it was difficult to run in the long robes. Tripping and stumbling, Gordon, Paulo and I ran down a dark ally, and then we suddenly stopped. We had run down a dead end! The ally ended in a high brick wall! We were trapped. We turned around in time to see the thieves coming toward us!

"Well, well, well! What have we here," said the first

thief with a menacing grin. "It looks like the Three Wise Men aren't so wise after all."

"Hand over the money and maybe you won't get hurt," snarled the second thief.

Gordon, Paulo and I stole quick glances at each other. I could tell by the look in their eyes that neither of them wanted to give up the money.

"No!" I shouted. "This money is for a poor family so they can give their kids a decent Christmas, and you're not going to take it!"

The thieves chuckled as they advanced slowly toward us. "Come on, kid. Play it smart. Hand over the money," said the first man.

"Yeah. Remember, it's better to give than to receive!" snarled the second man, shaking his powerful fist at Gordon.

"If you want it, come and get it," called Gordon, holding it out.

The thieves came closer and closer until they could

almost reach out and grab the box from Gordon's hands.

"NOW!" yelled Paulo, and he and I lunged at the men's legs, knocking them to the ground. The four of us fell in a tangled heap.

"RUN!" I yelled to Gordon. "Save the money!"

As Gordon started to run out of the alley, one of the thieves grabbed him by the ankle, bringing him down hard. We punched and kicked and struggled to get away from the men, but it was no use. They were big and powerful and we were no match for them. They ripped the cashbox out of Gordon's hands, leaving us on the ground. Not only had we lost the battle, we lost some poor family's only chance at a nice Christmas. I had never felt so unhappy and cheerless in my life.

As the thieves started running away with the cashbox, the alley was suddenly flooded with bright lights. The thieves stopped in their tracks as two police cars screeched to a halt, blocking their escape. Someone had noticed a strange car driving suspiciously through the neighbourhood and had called the police to investigate.

Thank goodness they arrived when they did!

The police wasted no time in handcuffing the thieves and putting them into the back of one of the cruisers. Then the officers approached the three of us, still wearing the Wise Men's costumes. Recognizing us despite the beards and robes, the first officer said,

"So, it's the Three Wise Men, eh? More like the Three Wise Guys!" and with that, we were tossed into the back of the second cruiser and driven to the police station.

"Somebody reported some vandalism over at the Church," said the officer. "They said the Three Wise Men had been stolen from the display on the lawn. I might have known it would be you three! You'll be charged with vandalism, assault, and theft!"

Gordon, Paulo and I sunk deep into the back seat and groaned. We were doomed. It looked like we were really in trouble this time, but when we got to the police station, we couldn't believe our luck! Fortunately for us, one of the policemen at the station had been at our school's charity dinner that night before coming on duty! We

45

quickly told the police officers what had happened.

The money was returned to Gordon, and the three of us were offered a ride home.

"I'm so glad you guys showed up when you did," Paulo told the police officers in the front seat.

"Yeah," agreed Gordon. "If you hadn't come along when you did, some poor kids would be getting nothing on Christmas morning."

Feeling happy and cheerful, we rode home in silence.

Chapter 6

First Impressions

In life, you only get one opportunity to introduce yourself to someone for the first time, and you should always try to make a good impression. Gordon, Paulo and I learned this the hard way. It had been raining for two days straight and we had spent both days at Gordon's house killing time waiting for the rain to stop so we could have some fun outside. The only bit of excitement was that a huge moving van had pulled up in front of the vacant house across the street from Gordon's and movers were busy carrying boxes into the house. Of course we knew it was not polite to stare at someone's stuff when they were moving in, so we were careful to stay out of sight and peek from behind the curtains to see what we could learn about the new people. Paulo and I soon grew tired of spying on the movers. You could only watch workmen unload chairs and sofas and lamps for so long. Gordon, however, sat out of sight behind the curtains staring across the street with his binoculars while Paulo and I watched TV.

"Hey!" said Gordon. "A car just pulled into the driveway. It must be the new people."

Paulo and I scrambled to the window just in time to see a man, a woman, a girl and a dog get out of the car and dash through the rain into their new house.

"Darn," sighed Gordon, tossing his binoculars onto the couch. "Well that's a disappointment. Another girl on the street. Why can't any boys our age ever move into the neighbourhood?"

As Gordon continued to gripe about the new girl, the rain let up and finally stopped. I interrupted Gordon to suggest that we get on our bikes and go to the corner store for some snacks.

"That's a great idea. I'm starving," said Paulo, and the three of us biked off to the store.

As we were heading back home, Gordon suddenly stopped and pointed up the street. "Look!" he said. "I think that's the new girl who just moved in. Why don't we be neighbourly and introduce ourselves?"

Up ahead I could see the new girl walking away from us toward her new house. She was carefully avoiding the puddles in the sidewalk. Spying the huge puddle on the road beside her, I suddenly knew what Gordon was up to. Pedalling hard on his bike, he made straight for the large puddle. With perfect timing, he raced his bike through it, sending up a huge plume of water on the unsuspecting girl, soaking her from head to foot.

"Hi! I'm Gordon!" he yelled as he rode by.

"And I'm Paulo!" shouted Paulo, imitating Gordon and splashing the girl again.

"And I'm....." But I never got the words out of my mouth. As my bike sent up a wall of water, the new girl startled me by jumping off the sidewalk and trying to tackle me off my bike. I was barely able to swerve out of the way in time. I sped off to catch up with Gordon and Paulo leaving the new girl in the middle of the road yelling at us.

"Talk about rude," chuckled Gordon when I'd caught up to him and Paulo. "She didn't even tell us her name!"

It began sprinkling again as we leaned our bikes against the wall in Gordon's garage, so we headed back into the house to watch TV and eat our snacks. About an hour later, the doorbell rang. Paulo peered out the window while Gordon went to answer the door.

"It's the new girl!" he hissed, and Paulo and I crept closer to listen.

Gordon opened the door and the new girl thrust a plate of freshly baked cookies into his hands.

"Here," she said. "I think we got off on the wrong foot earlier and I wanted to come over and introduce myself properly. After all, we are going to be neighbours. My name's Alex. I baked these for you guys."

"Uh, thanks," mumbled Gordon, too surprised to say much else.

"Oh, and one more thing," she said. "Here's a movie I made of my favourite TV shows. I thought you might enjoy it. I'm a big cartoon fan." She handed it to Gordon and headed back home through the rain.

"Well, what do you know? She might not be so bad after all," said Gordon. "And these cookies are pretty good!"

"Real good," said Paulo, munching on a handful. "Let's see what cartoons she likes."

While we enjoyed some really good classic cartoons, we finished off the cookies. Too stuffed to move, we watched one show after another, and then it happened. Abruptly, the cartoon we were watching cut out and suddenly Alex appeared on the screen. She was in a kitchen and she was baking. She was smiling at the camera as she rolled out the cookie dough on a breadboard. Then she set the breadboard on the floor and whistled. Into the kitchen bound a small dog, still damp

51

from the rain. Pointing to the breadboard, Alex said, "Sit!" and the little dog sat down, right in the middle of the cookie dough!

"Lie down!" commanded Alex, and the dog immediately obeyed.

"Roll!" said Alex, and the dog began rolling from side to side, scratching his back on the cookie dough.

"Good boy!" said Alex, scraping a handful of cookie dough from the dog's coat, which she added back to dough on the breadboard. She then proceeded to cut neat circles from the dough with a cookie cutter and smiling at the camera again, she put the batch of cookies into the oven to bake!

Chapter 7

The Surprise Party

It was June and there were just two weeks left of school. While we were excited about school ending soon, we were also wary; our teacher was working on our final report cards, and we all knew what teachers could be like during report card time. Everyone in class was on their best behaviour. As Gordon said, *'screw up now and whammo!'* Mrs. Hoagsbrith might get even by writing the twelve most dreaded words ever on a report card: *'Your child would benefit greatly by doing extra school work this summer.'* To ensure that this calamity didn't happen to any of us, Gordon came up with a foolproof plan. The class would buy Mrs. Hoagsbrith an end of the year present that we would give to our teacher before she signed the final copy of our report cards.

Gordon collected five dollars from each student and after school on Friday, the three of us, along with several other kids from our class, headed over to the mall.

"I wish I'd thought of this years ago," said Gordon. "When Mrs. H. gets our gift she'll be so choked up and touched she wouldn't dare put anything bad on our report cards."

I grinned. Nobody could fake sincerity like good ol' Gordon.

Everyone knew that our teacher loved and collected garden gnomes, so we headed straight for the garden centre, where we picked out an expensive, special limited-edition gnome. There was just enough money left over for a card.

We picked out a really sappy card with enough room for all of the kids to sign their names. The card said, *To the Greatest Woman in the World*. We were certain it would bring a tear to her eye.

Even though the gift had been Gordon's idea, no one trusted him not to accidentally break or lose the gnome, so I was elected to keep the gift safe at my house until Monday when we would present it to our teacher. I would bring the gift to school and everyone would sign the card at recess.

Arriving at my house before my parents got home from work, I took the box containing the garden gnome and the card up to my room and hid it under the bed for safe keeping.

The next morning I biked over to Paulo's house to help him feed the calf he was raising for the county fair. When I returned home for lunch, I could hear my mother running the vacuum upstairs. My lunch was sitting on the table so I sat down and dug in. And then it happened. Partway through my sandwich, the vacuum stopped and a few seconds later I could hear my mother crying. Startled, I ran up the stairs to eavesdrop. To my dismay, the crying was coming from my room! Oh, no! What had I done now?

55

I cautiously opened the door and saw my mother kneeling on the floor. The garden gnome stood beside her and she was holding the card we had bought for our teacher. She turned around when she heard me come into the room and exclaimed, "There you are, my sweet, sweet, darling boy!" She swept me into her arms and squeezed me until I could hardly breathe.

"I thought everyone had forgotten that today's my birthday! And all along you had this adorable gift and this lovely card hidden under your bed for me! I'm sorry I ruined your surprise, angel, but I was curious when my vacuum hit the box."

I was too stunned to speak. Before I could think of a way to let her down gently, she sighed and continued. "This is the nicest thing you've ever done for me. I just love this adorable garden gnome. I'll treasure it forever. And this is the most touching card anyone has ever given me."

She dabbed at her moist eyes. I had accidentally made my mom the happiest mother in the world! How could I tell her I had forgotten all about her birthday and that this gift was for my teacher?

Scooping up the garden gnome as though it were the Stanley Cup, she carried it downstairs and put it on display in the centre of the dining room table along with the card. I was doomed.

Since I couldn't possibly hurt my mother's feelings and tell her the truth, I decided that I would just have to buy another garden gnome and card for Mrs. Hoagsbrith with my own money.

I counted the money in my sock drawer and came up with eight dollars. I knew it was a long shot, but I phoned Paulo and told him what had happened, hoping he would have ninety-two dollars he could lend me. Unfortunately, he was more broke than I was. Gordon managed to scrape up twenty dollars when I phoned him, but it still wasn't nearly enough.

"What am I going to do?" I asked him over the phone. For once even Gordon didn't have a plan, but he said he would come right over and try to think of something.

Gordon arrived at the same time that my father and sister came in for lunch. When my sister saw the garden gnome and the card sitting on the dining room table, she said, "Hey, I thought we were waiting until dinner to give mom her presents!" She dashed upstairs and came back down with a box of chocolates.

"And my gift to you," my dad told my mother, "is that I am taking the whole family out for dinner to that new French restaurant you've been dying to try!"

My mother was thrilled. "And here I thought you'd all forgotten my birthday!" she said happily.

Gordon nudged me and whispered, "I've got an idea!"

I followed him up to my room where he closed the door and told me his plan. It was perfect!

Four hours later, my family, dressed in their best clothes, piled into the car and headed to the restaurant for my mother's birthday dinner. Before we left, I made sure that the back door was unlocked. I smiled to myself in the back seat. *Thank you, Gordon*, I thought. While my family was enjoying our fancy French dinner, Gordon was going to sneak into our house and steal the garden gnome out of our dining room!

"Your mom will be mad that her present was stolen, but at least she won't be broken-hearted, and you'll still get credit for giving her a really nice present!" Gordon had said. It was the only solution. With Gordon in charge, what could go wrong? Apparently plenty.

During dinner, when my mother excused herself to go to the ladies' room, my dad grinned and said he had a surprise for all of us. He hadn't told us earlier because he wasn't sure if my sister and I could keep a secret. He had planned a surprise party for my mother!

"Right about now," he said, looking at his watch, "guests are letting themselves into our house through the front door. I made sure it wasn't locked when we left. They'll be hiding, ready to jump out and yell 'Surprise!' the moment your mother walks through the front door!"

I couldn't speak. I knew our plan had sounded too easy. Gordon was going to get caught sneaking into my house and taking back the garden gnome! Everyone would think he was a thief. Gordon was going to kill me!

My mother returned from the ladies' room and my dad winked at my sister and me. I had suddenly lost my appetite. We finished our meal and headed home for my mother's surprise party.

When we turned onto our street, I was relieved to see that there were no cars parked on the road near our house. *Maybe no one's here yet*, I prayed. *Maybe Gordon slipped in through the back door, took the garden gnome and is already back home with it.* Of course, I wasn't that lucky. As our car pulled into the driveway, I spied Gordon's bike in the bushes where he'd hidden it. Oh, no, I thought. *We're* going to catch him in the act!

"Hey, mom! How about we all take a nice long walk around the neighbourhood?" I blurted out.

My father shot me an angry glance. "Not tonight," he snapped. "I'm beat. Let's go inside." He held the front door open for my mother, she stepped through, and thirty people jumped out from behind the furniture and drapes and yelled, "Surprise!!"

My mother screamed with delight and jumped back. Everyone laughed and shouted, "Happy birthday!" and the party began. I pushed my way through the crowd of guests and headed straight for the dining room. The garden gnome was gone and in its place stood a giant birthday cake with 'Happy 40th Birthday' written in pink icing. I began searching the house for Gordon. Where could he be hiding? I checked closets, the basement, under the beds and even outside, but there was no sign of him. He must have walked home with the gnome and left his bike in the bushes. I began to relax a little and enjoy the party. I ate two pieces of birthday cake and drank several glasses of punch. Before long, I needed to use the bathroom. There were several people waiting to use the bathroom ahead of me, and when it was finally my turn, I closed the door and locked it. I had just sat down on the toilet when a voice beside me made me jump in the air. Next to me the lid to the clothes hamper opened and out popped Gordon's head!

"Gordon!" I hissed. "What on earth are you doing in

61

our dirty clothes hamper?"

"What do you think I'm doing?" he hissed back. "I'm hiding! Why didn't you tell me about the party?"

"I didn't know!"

"Well, lucky for you I grabbed this just as the first guest came through the front door." He pulled out the garden gnome. "I barely had time to hide in the laundry hamper! And then more people arrived and I couldn't escape. Do you know how disgusting it is hiding in a dirty laundry hamper for two hours, especially with all those people coming in here and going to the bathroom right next to you?!"

"I'm really sorry, Gordon," I said, helping him out of the hamper and removing my dad's underwear from his head. I lowered Gordon from the bathroom window and carefully handed the gnome to him where he made his escape.

*   *   *   *   *

Later that night when the party was over and the guests had all gone home, my mom came into my room and sat on the edge of my bed.

"I'm afraid I have some really bad news for you, dear," she said. "One of the guests must have stolen the adorable garden gnome you gave me! I can't find it anywhere, and I really loved it. Oh, well, I'll always have the memory of the wonderful thing you did for me on my 40th birthday!"

Chapter 8

Buttons the Dog

"Buttons the dog!" said Gordon with disdain. "Who would actually name a dog 'Buttons'?"

Gordon, Paulo and I were at the mall in town, looking at the public bulletin board for easy jobs that would make us some money. We dreamed of finding jobs that would pay us to test new computer games or to try out new fishing lures or something equally fun, but all we found were jobs cutting grass, washing windows, and other equally hot and dirty work.

That's when Gordon spied the job of dog walking.

Someone was needed to walk Buttons the dog on Monday while his owner was out of town. The job paid twenty-five dollars.

"Twenty-five bucks just to walk a dog? Now that's my kind of job!" said Gordon, smiling. He took the notice down from the board and we went to the nearby payphone to dial the number. After four rings, an elderly-sounding man picked up the phone and said, "Yes?"

"Hello," said Gordon in his most responsible voice. "I'm calling about your ad for a dog walker."

"Oh, yes," replied the man. "I need someone to walk my dog for me on Monday while I'm out of town. My sister will come over and feed Buttons, but she's old and not up to walking him, even though he's a real gentle dog and wouldn't hurt a flea."

"Well," said Gordon. "My friends and I have lots of experience with pets. Last summer we watched our neighbour's cat. And we're all dog lovers!"

"Then the job is yours," said the old man. "I live in the green house at 14 Grey Street and I'll leave the key in the mailbox. All you have to do is come over at noon on Monday and walk Buttons around the block. His leash and collar are on the hook by the back door."

"That's great," said Gordon. "We'll be happy to walk Buttons for you!" He said good-bye and hung up the phone.

"The job's all ours!" declared Gordon as he left the phone booth. "We walk Buttons on Monday at noon. The guy lives in a grey house at 14 Green Street."

* * * * *

Just before noon on Monday, Gordon and Paulo met me at my house and we headed over to 14 Green Street. We found the grey house about half-way down the street, and just as the old man had said, the key was in the mailbox. We let ourselves in the front door and saw no sign of Buttons.

Gordon knelt down and called, "Here, Buttons! Come on, boy. We're going to take you for a walk!"

"Here, Buttons!" I called. And then it happened. Our only warning was a deep, rumbling growl from

66

somewhere in the basement, and then, bounding up the basement steps right toward us came the biggest, meanest looking, most ferocious dog I had ever seen! Gordon, Paulo and I instantly turned and dove back through the front door, slamming it shut just as the huge beast lunged toward us!

The three of us fell on the front porch in a tangled heap. Inside, we could hear the dog ramming against the door trying to get at us.

"Poor Buttons!" gasped Gordon. "That monster of a dog must have gotten into the house somehow and eaten little Buttons."

"Gordon, you idiot!" yelled Paulo. "That dog *is* Buttons! No wonder the old guy is paying so much to have someone walk his dog."

"That dog will kill us," I moaned. "What are we going to do?"

"I don't know about you guys," said Gordon, "but I want my share of that twenty-five bucks. And if we don't walk Killer, I mean Buttons, we won't get paid."

67

"But I don't want to get eaten alive in the process," I argued.

"Look on the bright side," grinned Gordon. "If you *are* eaten alive, my share of the twenty-five bucks will be that much bigger!"

Sometimes I wonder why I'm friends with Gordon at all.

We returned the key to the mailbox and biked back to my house to think of a plan.

"There has to be some way to walk that dog and not get bit," said Gordon. Suddenly he snapped his fingers. "I got it!" he said triumphantly. "Guys, let's get our hockey equipment and gear up!"

Although it was a blistering hot July day, Gordon, Paulo and I suited up with all of our padding, helmets, plastic protectors and gloves. On our feet we wore heavy socks and winter boots for protection. Grabbing some extra heavy ropes from the garage, we walked to Green Street and prepared to do battle with Buttons.

We arrived hot and sweaty at the grey house. Taking a

moment to catch our breath and gather our courage, we made three lassos out of the heavy rope we had brought. Our plan was to open the door, call Buttons, and lasso him around the neck when he lunged at us.

I turned the key in the lock and quietly opened the door. Buttons was nowhere in sight.

"Here, Buttons! Nice dog!" I called out. With saliva dripping from his jaws, Buttons roared out of the basement and charged up the stairs. I stepped back, and as the beast lunged toward us, Gordon and Paulo threw their lassos with all their might. They went right around the dog's thick neck! With Buttons somewhat distracted, I was able to get my lasso around him as well.

We figured that with three ropes on Buttons, we would be able to control him. We figured wrong. Buttons just fought harder! The only thing that saved us was our hockey equipment. Buttons took turns attacking each of us while the other two struggled to pull him off.

Our walk took on a strange rhythm: bite-fight-walk, bite-fight-walk until we had finally circled the block a single time. It took one hour. It was the hardest twenty-five dollars we had ever earned. Under my hockey pads I could feel large bruises beginning to swell.

It took another fifteen minutes of fighting and struggling to get the lassos off of Buttons. We finally succeeded and slammed the door shut behind us.

* * * * *

The next morning, Gordon, Paulo and I biked over to 14 Green Street to collect our money for walking Buttons. Gordon rang the bell and we waited for the old man to answer it. To our surprise, the door was opened by a young man.

"Can I help you?" he said.

"We're here to collect our money for walking Buttons yesterday," said Gordon.

"Buttons?" asked the man in a puzzled tone.

"Your um...dog," Paulo reminded him.

"My dog? You mean Sledgehammer?" he asked.

"Sledgehammer?" I repeated. "You mean that thing

70

that tried to kill us wasn't Buttons?"

The man laughed. "Buttons! What a silly name for a dog!"

"Didn't you hire us to walk your dog yesterday?" asked Gordon.

"Why would I do that?" he asked.

"We were told to come to the grey house at 14 Green Street and walk a dog named Buttons. The key was in the mailbox and everything!" explained Gordon.

"Oh, I see," said the man. "People are always making the same mistake. I think maybe you boys wanted the *green* house at 14 *Grey* Street. That's two blocks over. And I believe the man there does own a little dog. He's very friendly. I'm sure he'll be no trouble to walk." Chuckling to himself, he closed the door.

Chapter 9

The Petnapper

It was summer and everyone in town was talking about the latest rash of crimes. In the past three weeks, seven people had reported having their pets kidnapped and held for ransom. The police were at a loss to solve the crimes. They had no clue who the criminal might be or when he would strike next. No pet was safe and in order to ensure that the pet owner paid the ransom, along with the note came a terrifying picture of your pet. One kid from our class had his goldfish stolen out of his room while he was away at camp. When he returned home he found a ransom note. Attached to the note was a picture of his fish swimming in a toilet bowl. A man's hairy hand wearing a large diamond ring had one finger on the flusher warning what would happen if the ransom wasn't paid. An elderly lady down the street had her budgie stolen from its cage. A few days later a ransom note came in the mail along with a picture of her bird in a cage. Inches away from the cage sat a fat cat licking its chops! Even large animals weren't safe. At the farm across from Paulo's, a horse disappeared. When the ransom note arrived, it was accompanied by a picture of the hairy hand with the diamond ring holding up a bottle of glue. Everyone quickly paid the ransom to get their beloved pets back.

The police had been working on the case day and night for three weeks, but so far the only clue they had was that the petnapper had a hairy hand and wore a diamond ring. They had checked everyone in town with hairy hands and had found no one wearing a large diamond ring. Since they had no other clues, they decided to offer a reward to anyone who could catch the petnapper – a large reward:

$500.00.

Gordon, Paulo and I would have gladly turned the petnapper in for free had we known who he was, but with a $500.00 reward being offered, we were now very determined to catch the person kidnapping innocent pets.

A couple of days later while watching TV at Gordon's house, our favourite show was interrupted by a news bulletin. Another pet had been kidnapped; this time a dog. The dog was described as a small black dog with a short tail, last seen wearing a red collar. The dog answered to the name 'Buttons' and the owner was an elderly man living on Grey Street.

"Grey Street!" shouted Gordon. "That's the dog that we were hired to walk!"

"The poor old guy who owns Buttons must be worried sick," said Paulo.

"I'll bet Buttons is pretty scared, too," I added.

"What we need to do," said Gordon, "is look for a man with hairy hands wearing a big diamond ring."

"But the police have already searched the entire town for hairy-handed men with diamond rings. They found lots of hairy hands, but none with diamond rings," Paulo reminded him.

"I'll bet that's because the petnapper doesn't wear his diamond ring in public. He only wears it at home, which is where he takes all the pictures," insisted Gordon. "I'll bet he keeps his curtains closed, too, so no one sees him wearing his ring."

"And he must have a high fence around his yard so no one can see in," I added.

"Let's get our bikes and ride up and down every street in town," said Gordon. "We'll check out the houses with high fences and see if they also have their curtains drawn."

Paulo and I thought that was a great idea and the three of us hopped on our bikes and began riding up and down every street.

"We're almost done," announced Paulo after we'd been riding for over two hours. "The last street left is

Green Street."

"Hey," chuckled Gordon. "That's the street Sledgehammer lives on. That's one dog that will never be kidnapped!"

We turned our bikes onto Green Street and rode past the grey house where Sledgehammer lived. The curtains were wide open and the only fence was a short chain link one around the backyard.

We continued up the street, and when we got to the very last house, we stopped and stared at it. The curtains were drawn tight and there was a tall wooden fence around the entire yard.

"Well, well, well," said Gordon. "What have we here?"

"Listen," said Paulo. We could all hear soft music coming from the backyard. "Somebody's home. Let's knock on the door and see if a man with hairy hands answers!"

"Then we can tell the cops and collect our reward!" said Gordon.

We left our bikes at the foot of the driveway and walked to the front door. Paulo rang the bell. There was no answer so he knocked on the door. Still no one answered. We walked back to our bikes.

"Well," I said. "I guess we should go to the police anyway and tell them to check this place out."

"No," said Gordon. "They would laugh us right out of the police station! We need more evidence. We can't ask them to search a house just because it has a high fence and the curtains are drawn! What we need is some solid proof that the petnapper lives here."

"Right," agreed Paulo. "Somehow we have to see if a man with hairy hands lives here, and if so, we need to find out if he's wearing a big diamond ring. *Then* we can go to the police."

"And collect our reward," added Gordon with a grin. "I'm going to climb that tree beside the fence and spy into the backyard. You guys wait here and cover me."

As quietly as possible, Gordon climbed the tall tree and quickly disappeared amongst the leaves. A moment later he whispered loudly, "Guys! Get up here quick!"

Paulo and I scampered up the tree. Silently Gordon pointed to a man in the backyard. He was lying on a lounge chair beside a pool with his eyes closed, half-asleep, and on his hairy hand, glistening in the sun, was a large diamond ring. Lying under the lounge chair tied by a leash was Buttons the dog!

"Great!" whispered Paulo. "Let's get down from here and go get the police."

"No," argued Gordon. "We have to rescue Buttons first. Then we'll call the cops. I've got a plan."

Paulo and I looked at each other, but we knew it was useless to argue with Gordon when he had a plan.

"OK," sighed Paulo. "Let's hear it."

"I've been watching this guy, and every couple of minutes he drops his hand and pats Buttons on the head. Then Buttons licks the guy's hand, and he folds his arms across his chest again and goes back to sleep. That gives us about two minutes between pats to sneak in through the gate and rescue Buttons."

Paulo and I watched, and sure enough, in a couple of
minutes, the man reached down with his hairy hand and
patted Buttons on the head. The dog licked the man's
hand and then he folded them across his chest again.

"See," said Gordon. "That gives us two minutes to
rescue Buttons. By the time the hairy guy figures out
what happened, we'll be out of sight and have Buttons
halfway home by then."

I wasn't crazy about the idea, but I couldn't think of a
better one, so we agreed to give it a try. After all, what
was the worst thing that could happen?

Paulo stayed in the tree watching the petnapper in
order to give Gordon the signal. When he raised his
thumbs, Gordon and I would sneak into the backyard.

A few minutes later, Paulo gave the thumbs up signal
and Gordon and I slowly opened the gate and crawled on
our bellies toward the sleeping man. Slithering under the
lounge chair, Gordon quickly undid the leash and I
snatched the little dog. And then it happened. Before I
could put my hand over the dog's muzzle to keep him

from barking and giving us away, Buttons let out a little whimper. The petnapper's hand came down to give him a reassuring pat on the head, but I had already started back across the yard with Buttons held tightly in my arms. Thinking fast, Gordon shoved his head under the man's hairy hand. The petnapper patted Gordon on the head. Then the man held his hand down waiting for it to be licked. Closing his eyes and grimacing, Gordon licked the man's hairy hand! Reassured that all was OK, the petnapper folded his arms across his chest and dozed off.

Gordon crawled back to the gate where I waited with Buttons. Just as Gordon was closing the gate, the wind caught it and it shut with a loud bang! Instantly, the petnapper was awake and on his feet.

"Go!" shouted Gordon, and we started to run with the little dog tucked safely under my arm. Stealing a quick glance behind me, I could see the petnapper in hot pursuit. For a big hairy man, he could really run!

"Follow me!" shouted Gordon, heading down Green Street and toward the familiar grey house where

Sledgehammer, the beast we had mistakenly walked, lived. Would we make it in time? The petnapper was only a house-length behind us and gaining quickly. At last, we got to Sledgehammer's house. Paulo was waiting on the front porch. In his hand was the key that we knew was kept hidden in the mailbox. As Gordon and I charged across the front lawn with Buttons, Paulo stuck the key in the door and turned the handle. Gordon, Paulo, and I burst into the house. As expected, Sledgehammer was sleeping in the basement. When he heard the commotion, he charged upstairs snapping and growling. By the time he reached the top of the stairs, we had already run through the house and slammed the back door shut behind us. Peeking through the back window of the house, we watched the petnapper burst through the front door in pursuit.

"Get out of my way, mutt!" bellowed the petnapper foolishly as he kicked at Sledgehammer. The dog effortlessly caught the kicking foot in his mouth and bit down hard! The petnapper roared in pain. He was big and strong but he was no match for Sledgehammer, who kept attacking until at last the petnapper tore free and dove into a bedroom, slamming the door shut in Sledgehammer's face. The dog continued to bark and growl at the closed door, trapping the man inside. Gordon, Paulo and I grinned at each other. We had saved Buttons and trapped the petnapper! Now all we had to do was return Buttons to his owner, call the police and collect our reward!

No one was home when we arrived at Buttons' house, so we carefully dropped the little dog into his fenced backyard. We headed back to Green Street where we would phone the police from a neighbour's house. To our surprise, when we got there, three police cars were already there with their lights flashing. The petnapper was being led away in handcuffs, his diamond ring sparkling in the sun! We heard Sledgehammer's owner talking to the police.

"It's just like I told you, Officer. I came home from work and found my front door open. I noticed a torn green shirt in my dog's mouth. I found a large man cowering under my bed crying, *'Keep your dog away!'* so I called 911."

"Well," the police chief said, "I guess the $500.00 reward is yours, and I hope you and Seldgehammer enjoy it. You're both heroes. Thanks for helping us catch the petnapper!"

Chapter 10

Mr. Butterworth's Bad Day

It was August and Gordon, Paulo and I had just spent the entire afternoon at Paulo's house playing in the barn. We worked for hours arranging bales of hay into a series of tunnels, hidden rooms and a lookout. It was the best hay fort we had ever made and we had worked up quite an appetite. We headed into the kitchen of the farmhouse looking for a quick snack. It was close to dinnertime, and knowing how every mother feels about kids "ruining their supper," we snuck in and quietly lifted the lid off of the cookie jar. We each grabbed a handful of the huge homemade cookies and were just tiptoeing out of the kitchen when Paulo's mother burst through the door.

"There you are!" she blurted out, completely ignoring the cookies in our hands. "I've been looking everywhere for you. Have you heard the news?"

"No," we said in unison.

"We've been in the barn all afternoon," added Paulo.

We had learned long ago that there were two types of news: good news (where nobody gets in trouble) and bad news (where somebody always gets in trouble, usually Gordon, Paulo and me). We all stared at Mrs. Lima, trying to determine which type of news this was.

To my surprise, she rushed up to me and put her hand on my shoulder. "Your mother phoned a few minutes ago. It seems that an ambulance has taken your neighbour to the hospital. I know how fond you are of Mr. Butterworth."

I was too shocked to speak. *Poor Mr. Butterworth*, I thought.

"He was out cutting his grass and he fell and hit his head," she continued. "He was knocked unconscious."

"Is he going to be OK?" asked Paulo.

"It's too soon to tell," said his mother. "He's not a young man..." She didn't need to finish her sentence.

The three of us sat down at the kitchen table to eat our cookies, but our appetites seemed to have vanished.

"He'll be OK," said Paulo, trying to cheer me up. "He's a tough old guy."

"I think we should visit him at the hospital tomorrow if they'll let him have visitors," said Gordon. "After all, he's been pretty good to us."

"That's a great idea," I said. Mr. Butterworth *had* been good to the three of us and we were all quite concerned for him.

The next morning Paulo and Gordon arrived at my house wearing their best clothes. Like me, their shoes were polished, their hair was combed and they were freshly showered. Gordon even wore a tie. We wanted to look our very best for the visit and we all clutched Get Well cards in our hands. My mother drove us to the small hospital in town and dropped us off at the door marked

86

"Visitor Entrance".

"I'll pick you up in half an hour," she told us.

Inside the hospital, Gordon, Paulo and I hurried to the front desk and asked where Mr. Butterworth's room was. A hospital volunteer in a striped jumper told us it was on the third floor, room 317.

When the elevator door finally opened on the third floor, we made our way to the nurse's station to ask whether Mr. Butterworth could have visitors. The station was deserted. We looked down the long hall leading to the patients' rooms. It too was deserted, so we decided to go straight to room 317 and quietly peek inside.

The door was slightly ajar when we found Mr. Butterworth's room. We peeked inside. Mr. Butterworth was lying in bed and the light was off. I gently knocked on the door, and when there was no answer, I quietly called his name. Again there was no response, so Gordon, Paulo and I tiptoed into his room to leave our Get Well cards on his bedside table where he would find them when he awoke.

Poor Mr. Butterworth lay motionless in the hospital bed, his head wrapped in a large bandage, monitors humming beside him and tubes coming out of his nose and mouth. We crossed the room and stood beside his bed, looking down on the sleeping old man, and then it happened.

Suddenly, Mr. Butterworth's eyes flew open and he made a horrible gasping sound as he struggled to breathe! He sat up in bed, waving his arms about frantically.

Thank goodness we had arrived when we did! Paulo and I were too stunned to move, but Gordon leapt into action.

"I'll get a nurse!" he shouted, running out of the room. As he did, Mr. Butterworth managed to get a breath of air and he seemed to relax a little. He fell back on the pillows gasping heavily. Beads of sweat had formed on his forehead and were soaking into his bandage.

Seconds later, Gordon raced back into the room and ran up to the bedside. "I can't find anyone!" he shouted.

I opened my mouth to tell Gordon that Mr. Butterworth